# The Never Girls

# a dandelion wish

Written by
## Kiki Thorpe

Illustrated by

# Parragon

Bath · New York · Cologne · Melbourne · Delhi
Hong Kong · Shenzhen · Singapore · Amsterdam

This edition published by Parragon Books Ltd in 2014

Parragon Books Ltd
Chartist House
15–17 Trim Street
Bath BA1 1HA, UK
www.parragon.com

ISBN 978-1-4723-3130-4

Printed in UK

# Never Land

Far away from the world we know, on the distant seas of dreams, lies an island called Never Land. It is a place full of magic, where mermaids sing, fairies play and children never grow up. Adventures happen every day, and anything is possible.

There are two ways to reach Never Land. One is to find the island yourself. The other is for it to find you. Finding Never Land on your own takes a lot of luck and a pinch of fairy dust. Even then, you will only find the island if it wants to be found.

Every once in a while, Never Land drifts close to our world … so close a fairy's laugh slips through. And every once in an even longer while, Never Land opens its doors to a special few. Believing in magic and fairies from the bottom of your heart can make the extraordinary happen. If you suddenly hear tiny bells or feel a sea breeze where there is no sea, pay careful attention. Never Land may be nearby. You could find yourself there in the blink of an eye.

Torth Mountain

Pixie Hollow

SKULL ROCK

Mermaid Lagoon

One day, four special girls came to Never Land in just this way. This is their story.

# Chapter 1

Mia Vasquez awoke one Saturday morning with a fluttery feeling in her chest. A feeling that something great awaited her that day.

She rubbed her eyes, trying to recall what it was. Then she remembered: *Never Land.*

The two words sent her leaping from her bed. She ran to the window and looked out at the back garden. White clouds chased each other across the blue sky. The grass was tall and the flowers bloomed in their beds. But it was the high wooden fence that held Mia's attention.

The day before, Mia, her little sister, Gabby, and her friends Kate and Lainey had discovered that by crawling through a loose board in the fence, they could reach the magical island of Never Land. No one knew how the passage between the two worlds had come to be – not even the fairies whose magic had brought the girls to Never Land in the first place. But to Mia it was a dream come true. To think she could visit the fairy world any time she wanted, just by going through the fence in her own garden!

Mia dressed quickly in a polka-dot skirt and her favourite pink T-shirt. Her long, curly black hair fell over her shoulders. She considered a pretty pair of sandals, then pulled on her trainers instead. Trainers were better for adventures – and there were always adventures to be had in Never Land.

When she was dressed, Mia hurried downstairs to the kitchen. She poured herself a bowl of cereal and slid into a chair next to her little sister. Gabby was wearing a pink tutu and a pair of fairy wings – her everyday outfit. She was drawing a picture of a fairy with crayons.

The girls' mother was standing at the kitchen counter, drinking a cup of coffee. "That's a nice drawing, Gabby," she said. "What's the fairy's name?"

"That's Tinker Bell," Gabby said. "She lives in Pixie Hollow."

Mrs Vasquez smiled. "Where is that?"

"It's on the other side of the – ow! Mia!" Gabby exclaimed as Mia kicked her under the table. When she caught Gabby's eye, Mia frowned and shook her head. Their parents didn't know about Never Land and Mia didn't want them to find out. She had a feeling that if they did, the girls' adventuring would be over.

Through the kitchen window, Mia could see her father working in the garden. She hoped he would be done soon. Otherwise, they wouldn't be able to sneak through the fence.

"Is Papi going to be working in the garden for long?" Mia asked her mother casually. "Kate and Lainey are coming over. We were going to, um … play outside."

"Your friends can't come over today, Mia," her mother said. "I'm going out to do some errands and I need you to look after Gabby."

"What? But I already told them they could come!" Mia cried.

"You'll have to call them and tell them they can't," her mother replied.

And not go to Never Land? Mia couldn't bear the thought. "Can't they come over anyway?" she asked. "We can all watch Gabby together."

"No, Mia," said her mum. "If you get busy playing with your friends, you'll forget to keep an eye on Gabby."

"I wouldn't!" Mia said. She thought about the first time they'd found themselves in Never Land, pulled there on a fairy's blink. Hadn't she and her friends taken good care of Gabby then? But, of course, she couldn't point this out to her mother.

"Kate and Lainey can come over another time," Mrs Vasquez said.

"It's not fair!" Mia complained. "Papi's here. Why can't he watch Gabby?"

"Papi is busy today. Mia, please don't sulk. It's just one day. You're old enough to be responsible."

"Who cares about being responsible?" Mia grumbled under her breath. She watched, arms folded, as her mother picked up her handbag and left.

When she was gone, Mia called Kate and Lainey and told them they couldn't come over. Then she returned to the table, plopped herself down in a chair, and glared at her sister.

Gabby didn't seem to notice. "Do you want to play a game?"

"No," Mia snapped.

"Do you want to colour?" asked Gabby.

Mia's frown deepened. "No. Why don't you go watch TV or something?"

"I'm not supposed to watch TV unless Mami says it's okay," Gabby pointed out.

"Well, I'm in charge today, and *I* say it's okay," Mia replied.

At once, Gabby hopped up from the table. She ran into the living room. A moment later, Mia heard the television turn on.

With nothing better to do, Mia followed. She flopped down on the sofa. On the television screen, a bunch of cartoon monsters were singing a silly song.

Mia sighed. She couldn't think of anything more frustrating than to be stuck watching a lame kids' show when she could be spending time with *real* fairies.

She looked out of the living room window at the high wooden fence. Never Land lay just on the other side. She could reach it in less than 30 seconds.

*Well, why shouldn't I?* Mia thought. *I could just pop over and see what's going on in Pixie Hollow. I'll be back before anyone even knows I'm gone.*

Mia glanced at her sister. Gabby was caught up in her cartoon. *She'll be fine for a few minutes,* Mia thought.

Quietly, she slipped off the sofa and let herself out of the back door.

She didn't see her father, but she could hear him whistling. He was working somewhere round the side of the house. Now was her chance.

The loose board was on the fence that separated their garden from their neighbour's. Mia had to spend a few moments nudging the boards until she found the right one. The board swung sideways on its nail, creating a gap just big enough for her to squeeze through.

As Mia knelt down, she felt a warm breeze on her face. She could smell jasmine and sun-warmed moss – the sweet scents of Pixie Hollow. She took a deep breath, then crawled through the opening, pulling the board back into place behind her.

*

She came out of a hollow tree into a sun-dappled forest. To her left was a wildflower-filled meadow. To her right, Havendish Stream burbled between its banks. And just beyond the stream lay Pixie Hollow. Mia could see fairies darting through the air as they flew to and from the giant Home Tree.

Mia heard a commotion downstream. She followed the sound round a bend to a small wooden bridge. Dozens of fairies swarmed around the bridge. They carried rope and bits of wood and buckets full of sand.

Mia saw Tinker Bell flying past. "Hi, Tink. What's going on?" she asked.

"The footbridge is broken," Tink replied. Mia saw that part of the bridge had collapsed into the stream. "We think Bingo must have smashed it when he was chasing fairies."

"Oh no!" Bingo was Mia's cat. The day before, he'd slipped through the fence into Never Land and caused trouble. "Can you fix it?"

"Yes, but it will take a lot of work," Tink said happily. "I'd better get back." She waved to Mia and flew off. Tink was always happiest when she had something to fix.

The fairies at the bridge all seemed busy, too, so Mia decided to go to the Home Tree. Perhaps she could find someone to talk to there.

In the pebbled courtyard, Mia saw sweeping-talent fairies tidying up.

They waved to Mia, but kept on with their jobs. It was the same in the kitchen. When Mia peered through the tiny doorway, the cooking- and baking-talent fairies barely looked up.

"Busy day in Pixie Hollow," said the baking fairy Dulcie as she rolled out pie dough. "Lots of hungry fairies to feed."

Mia was disappointed. She'd hoped she might come upon a tea party or a game of fairy tag. But everyone in Pixie Hollow was hard at work. Mia wondered if she should help – after all, it was her cat that had caused the mess. But she knew she shouldn't leave Gabby alone for too long. Time worked differently in Never Land, and Mia couldn't be sure if a minute or an hour had gone by since she had left.

As Mia started back, she passed a tiny house made from a gourd that sat on one of the Home Tree's lowest branches. She tapped on the little wooden door with her finger.

The garden fairy Rosetta opened the door. She was dressed in a glorious ruffled gown made from a pink carnation. "Mia!" Rosetta exclaimed. "I was hoping someone might drop by. I'm glad it's you!"

"Are you going to a party?" Mia asked hopefully, eyeing Rosetta's fancy dress.

Rosetta sighed sadly. "No parties today – not even a picnic. Everyone is too busy cleaning up after … well, you know, what happened with Bingo."

"Why aren't you busy, too?" asked Mia.

"Well, Bingo made a great mess of almost everything, but he left all the flowers alone. There's not much for a garden fairy to do. So I've been trying on dresses. Sometimes I do that when

I'm feeling bored," Rosetta admitted. "But now I'm out of dresses – I've tried on everything!"

Suddenly, Mia had an idea. It was such a good idea that she wondered why she hadn't thought of it before. "Why don't you come to my house? I have lots of dresses that would fit you perfectly," she said, thinking of her doll's clothes.

"You mean, go through the hollow tree to the mainland? I don't know." Rosetta suddenly looked nervous. "Some fairies say it's dangerous."

Mia laughed. "It's not dangerous. I just came through it! Rosetta, you have to come. I have a pink velvet dress that would look beautiful on you. Oh! And one made of blue lace. And a green one with a little matching bag...."

As Mia described the dresses, Rosetta's blue eyes widened. At last, she burst out, "I'd love to see them all!"

"Come on. Let's go right now," said Mia.

With Rosetta flying beside her, Mia led the way back to the hollow tree. She was thrilled. This was the perfect answer to her problem. She could look after Gabby and still have fun!

But when they got to the tree, Rosetta hesitated. "Are you sure it's safe?" she asked.

"You can ride in my pocket, if it makes you feel better," Mia said.

Rosetta flew into Mia's pocket. Then Mia crawled into the hollow tree, and went back to her own world.

# chapter 2

As Mia came back through the fence into her garden, she could still hear her father whistling round the side of the house. *Good,* Mia thought. That meant she'd only been gone for a few moments.

Quickly, Mia crossed the garden and went in the back door to the house. "I'll be in my room, Gabby," she said as she passed the living room.

Gabby looked up from the television. "What's that?" she asked, eyeing the lump in Mia's pocket.

"Nothing. Mind your own business," Mia said, hurrying up the stairs to her room.

In the hallway, Bingo was prowling. When he saw Mia, he wrapped himself round her legs and purred. Inside the pocket, Rosetta tensed.

"Go away, Bingo." Mia nudged the cat gently with her foot. She slipped past him into her room, quickly shutting the door behind her. On the other side, Bingo yowled in protest.

"It's okay," Mia said to Rosetta. "You can come out now."

Rosetta wriggled out of the pocket. "Phew!" She fluffed her long red hair. Then her eyes widened, and she gave a little gasp. "Oh my!"

Mia glanced around, seeing her room through Rosetta's eyes. Instantly, she regretted not making her bed that morning. And all those clothes on the floor – why hadn't she noticed them before?

Mia hastily scooped up socks and T-shirts, threw them in the laundry basket and yanked the purple duvet up over her bed. But when Mia glanced back at Rosetta, she realized the fairy wasn't looking at the mess. She was staring, transfixed, at the corner of the room, where a large doll's house stood.

Rosetta flew over and landed in the doll's house living room. She examined the little sofa, the miniature grandfather clock and the postage-stamp pictures on the walls. Her fairy glow cast a warm light over the small room, making it look as if the doll's house lamps were lit.

Moving from room to room, Rosetta explored the rest of the doll's house.

She touched the tiny china teacups in the dining room. She opened the oven door in the kitchen. She even stretched out on the four poster bed in the guest bedroom.

Mia's breath caught in delight. She had always liked playing with her doll's house, but it had never been more than a pretty toy. The moment the fairy stepped inside, though, the house came to life.

"Who lives here?" Rosetta asked.

"No one," Mia replied. "It's … just for fun."

"Just for fun?" Rosetta cried in surprise. "But it's a perfect home for a fairy!"

Mia grinned, imagining a fairy living in her doll's house.

At that moment, the door to Mia's room burst open. Gabby stood in the doorway. "I knew it!" she crowed, spying Rosetta. "I knew you had a fairy here!"

"Gabby!" cried Mia. "You're supposed to knock!"

Gabby ignored her. She barged into the room. "What are you guys playing? Can I play, too? Will you come to my room, Rosetta? I want to show you my toys and my books and my stuffed animals. Can you come right now? Can you?"

Mia grabbed hold of her sister by one of the wings she was wearing and spun her round. "Out!" she yelled. "Get out of my room!"

"Let go, Mia!" Gabby shouted.

"It's all right, Mia," Rosetta said. She flew out of the doll's house, which became just an ordinary toy once again.

"No, it's not," Mia said. "It's my room, and I didn't invite Gabby in. She's *intruding*." Mia knew she was being mean, but she couldn't stop herself.

Gabby was the reason she was stuck at home and not in Never Land. Even though Mia knew it wasn't Gabby's fault, she couldn't help being mad at her.

As the sisters glared at each other, a blur of brown fur streaked into the room through the open door.

"Bingo!" the girls shrieked. They dived for the cat at the same time. Their heads collided with a loud smack. Bingo shot past them, heading right for Rosetta.

The fairy screamed and darted into the air. Bingo leaped on to Mia's chest of drawers. He stood on his hind legs, batting the air as he tried to reach the fairy.

Gabby jumped up to grab him, but she wasn't quite tall enough. Instead, she knocked Mia's jewellery box off the chest of drawers. The box crashed to the floor and the hinges broke.

All the trinkets fell out and scattered across the floor.

"Gabby!" Mia wailed. "Bingo!" Mia didn't know who to yell at first. She snatched the cat off her chest of drawers and tucked him under her arm. Then she clamped her other hand on Gabby's shoulder, steering her towards the door. "Both of you – out!"

"I want to stay!" Gabby said, digging in her heels.

"No. You mess up *everything*," Mia said. She pushed Gabby and Bingo into the hall and locked the door behind them.

"Fine! Then I'll do something fun in *my* room. And *you're* not invited!" Gabby shouted through the door.

"Fine with me!" Mia shouted back.

Gabby stomped away. A second later, Mia heard her bedroom door slam.

"I don't think she meant to let Bingo in," Rosetta said, fluttering down from the ceiling.

Mia touched her head. It throbbed where she'd run into Gabby. "You don't know what it's like to have a little sister," she told Rosetta. "Gabby's always getting in the way."

"Maybe I should go home," the fairy said. She looked nervous and Mia realized she was still afraid of Bingo.

"Don't leave yet!" Mia begged. If Rosetta left now, the whole day would be ruined. "I haven't even shown you the dresses!"

Mia hurried to her wardrobe and pulled out the two shoe boxes where she kept her doll's clothes. She lifted the lids and began laying the dresses out one by one.

Pink, yellow, green, gold. Satin, taffeta and lace. Some of the dresses were trimmed with ribbon, others were puffed up by petticoats. Some even had matching cloaks and hats.

Rosetta came closer, lured by the lovely clothes. "Look how many there are!"

"Try one on," Mia urged.

"All right. Just one." After much consideration, Rosetta selected a ruffled pink dress with a gold sash.

The dress fitted perfectly. Rosetta flew back and forth in front of Mia's mirror, admiring herself. Mia clapped her hands. The dress had never looked this pretty on her dolls. "Try this one next!" she urged, holding up a yellow ball gown.

Rosetta tried on dress after dress.

Mia thought each one looked lovelier than the last. She was having so much fun she didn't notice time passing.

*Bang! Bang! Bang!* A pounding sound from outside startled Mia.

"What was that?" asked Rosetta.

"I don't know." Suddenly, Mia thought of Gabby. How long had it been since she'd seen her? "I'll be right back," she told Rosetta.

Mia went across the hall. But Gabby's room was empty. Downstairs, the television was still on, but Gabby wasn't watching. She wasn't in the kitchen or the bathroom either.

Mia went back to her room. "I can't find her," she told Rosetta.

"Who?" asked the fairy. She had on a green satin dress and was admiring herself in the mirror.

"Gabby!" exclaimed Mia. "She's not anywhere in the house."

Rosetta looked at her. "Where else could she be?"

With a sinking feeling, Mia suddenly knew exactly where her sister was.

Gabby had gone through the fence into Pixie Hollow!

"Gabby, you're such a pest," she grumbled to herself. But she hurried down the stairs. It was one thing for Mia to go to Never Land on her own, but Gabby was just a little girl. Who knew what kind of trouble she could get into?

When she stepped outside, Mia spotted Gabby's jumper, the one she'd been wearing that morning. It was lying on the ground near the fence. Mia knew then that she was right. Gabby must have taken it off before she went through the hole.

Mia saw her father standing at the fence. He had a hammer in his hand. But what was he doing?

As Mia watched, her father brought the hammer down on the fence. *Bang! Bang! Bang!*

"Oh no!" Mia cried. Her father was fixing the hole in the fence – and Gabby was on the other side!

# Chapter 3

Iridessa, a light-talent fairy, knelt before a pool of sunlight. She reached into the pool and pulled out a sunbeam. Her hands shaped the beam into a ball, like a golden glowing pearl. Then she placed it in her basket.

Iridessa sat back on her heels and eyed the basket of sunbeams. It was almost full. *Is that enough?* she wondered.

*Better get a few more,* she decided. In Iridessa's opinion, it was always better to be safe than sorry. With the bridge builders working through the night, Pixie Hollow would need extra light.

As soon as she was done collecting sunbeams, she needed to round up more fireflies. There was so much to do! Luckily, Iridessa had made a plan for the day. She glanced up at the sun high in the sky and smiled. She was right on schedule.

Iridessa reached into the pool again. But just as her fingers touched it, a shadow fell over her.

She turned. A giant loomed above. Iridessa noticed that it had wings – and a tutu. "Gabby?" she said.

"Hi, Iridessa." The girl squatted down next to her. "Will you come to my room? I'm having a party."

"Now?" Iridessa wondered why anyone would have a party at such a busy time.

"Everyone is invited – except Mia," Gabby told her.

Suddenly, Iridessa understood. "Did you have a fight with your sister?"

Gabby's forehead furrowed. "She won't let me play with her and Rosetta. And she yelled at me, even though it wasn't my fault about Bingo. And she made me leave. She pulled my wings! She's mean!"

Iridessa didn't know what to make of all this. But she did know what it was like to be mad at someone. "Perhaps she wasn't mean on purpose," she said.

"She was so," said Gabby. "I never want to see her again."

"Come now," said Iridessa. "There must be something you like about your sister."

Gabby shook her head.

"Think hard," Iridessa urged. "Just one thing."

Gabby considered. "Well, sometimes she lets me watch TV."

"What is that?" asked the fairy.

Gabby looked at her in amazement. "It's ... TV!"

*Some quaint Clumsy custom, no doubt,* thought Iridessa. "Well, imagine if you didn't have your sister *or* TV. Wouldn't that be sad?"

"I guess so," said Gabby.

"I'll bet if you remind Mia how much you like it when you watch TV, it will make her feel happy. And then you two can make up," Iridessa said.

"Do you really think so?" Gabby asked.

"Yes," said Iridessa. "People always like to hear good things about themselves. Sometimes the best way to get over an argument is to remember the nice things about each other. You should talk to Mia. Come on, I'll take you back to the hollow tree."

Iridessa picked up her basket of sunbeams. This wasn't part of her day's plan, but she was glad to help. Iridessa liked to see things sorted out. And it had only taken her – Iridessa glanced at the sun – 47 seconds!

She led Gabby across the meadow and back to the tree that held the portal to the girls' world. Iridessa stopped at the entrance to the hollow.

"Fly safely," she said in the typical fairy manner.

"Okay." Gabby turned and ducked into the hollow. But a second later, she came back out.

"What's wrong?" Iridessa asked.

"The hole isn't there," said Gabby.

"Of course it is," Iridessa replied. "You came through it earlier, didn't you?"

Gabby nodded. "But now it's gone."

Iridessa thought Gabby must be mistaken. She set down her basket and flew into the tree. It was dark inside the hollow, but all fairies glow a little and Iridessa's glow was stronger than most. She could see the inside walls of the hollow, smooth and unbroken.

"It's gone! The portal's gone!" Iridessa exclaimed, flying out of the tree.

"I told you," said Gabby.

"What should I do?" Iridessa asked. This was important news! But whether it was good or bad news, Iridessa wasn't certain. She fluttered back and forth. She sometimes got flustered when things didn't work out as planned.

Just then, a messenger-talent fairy flew by. Iridessa zipped over and told her what they'd discovered. Within moments, the messenger had spread the news around Pixie Hollow. Fairies and sparrow men all stopped what they were doing. They came to examine the tree.

"So it's true?" asked Queen Clarion, flying over.

"It is," said Tinker Bell, who'd been inspecting the tree. "The hollow is still there. But the portal has vanished!"

As the fairies buzzed with the news, Iridessa's eyes darted to Gabby. The girl stood off to the side, watching the fairies silently. She seemed to be waiting to be told what to do. The other fairies barely noticed her, however. They were all focused on the tree.

Iridessa flew over to Queen Clarion. "What about Gabby?" she murmured. "She can't get home. Someone will need to look after her."

The queen rubbed a hand across her forehead. She looked distracted. "Yes, you're right, of course. That's very good of you, Iridessa."

"What? Oh! No." Iridessa shook her head and tried to explain. "That's not

what I meant...." But the queen was already flying away.

Iridessa sighed. She had sunbeams to collect and fireflies to gather. Looking after a Clumsy was *not* part of her plan.

She flew back over to Gabby. "Don't worry," she said brightly. "I'm sure the hole will open again in no time." Iridessa wasn't sure of any such thing, but she didn't want Gabby to worry.

In the meantime, she had no choice. If she was going to stick to her plan, she'd just have to bring Gabby along with her.

*Well, she's only a young girl, after all,* she thought. *How hard can it be to look after her?*

# chapter 4

Mia ran towards her father, crying, "Papi, wait!"

Mr Vasquez looked up. "Mia?"

When she reached the fence, Mia ran her fingers along it. None of the boards budged. "There was a loose board!"

"I know, I fixed it," her father replied. "I've been meaning to repair this old fence for ages. You don't know what might get through a hole like that. Stray dogs or cats or – Mia, honey, what's the matter?"

"Gabby is...." Mia trailed off, her mind racing.

What if she told her father about Never Land? What would happen? Would he tell other grown-ups about the fairy world? Would he leave the hole sealed up for good? Would he even believe her?

Mia didn't know. But one thing was certain – if her parents found out she'd lost Gabby, she was going to be in big trouble.

Her father frowned. "Gabby is what?"

"Sleeping," Mia said quickly, making a decision. "She's taking a nap. I was afraid the hammering would wake her up."

"Well, I'm done here." Her father picked up his tools. "I've got some work to do in the garage. *Quiet* work," he added with a wink. Then he patted Mia's cheek.

"You're a good big sister."

A guilty lump rose in Mia's throat. She swallowed hard, forcing it down. *It's not my fault,* Mia told herself. *If Gabby hadn't left without telling me, this wouldn't have happened!*

When her father was gone, Mia turned back to the fence. She tried wiggling the wooden boards. Then she tried kicking them. But not one of them budged.

"Stupid fence!" Mia exclaimed, giving it an extra kick.

"Mia?" said a voice behind her.

Mia turned and saw Rosetta hovering. She was still wearing the green satin doll's dress. "What's going on?" the fairy asked.

Gabby wasn't the only one who was trapped in the wrong world, Mia realized. Rosetta was stuck, too!

But unlike Gabby, Rosetta had magic. Maybe she could help. "Papi fixed the fence. But Gabby is in Never Land and now she can't get home!" Mia explained. "Can you do something?"

"You mean, the way back to Never Land is gone?" Rosetta's face turned pale. Her eyelids fluttered. Mia stuck out her hand just in time to catch her as she fainted.

*

Inside the house, Mia ran a towel under the kitchen tap. Carefully, she squeezed a drop of water on to Rosetta's forehead.

The fairy spluttered and sat up. When she saw Mia's giant face hovering over her, she screamed.

Mia backed away quickly. "Sorry! I didn't mean to scare you."

Rosetta put a hand to her cheek. "What happened?"

"You fainted when I told you we can't get back to Never Land," Mia said.

Rosetta looked like she might faint again, so Mia made her comfortable on a dry kitchen sponge.

"That's better. A cup of tea would be nice, too," Rosetta said.

Mia didn't know how to make tea. But she wanted Rosetta to feel better. She fetched a doll's teacup from her room and put a drop of fizzy drink in it, then handed it to the fairy.

Rosetta took one sip and yelped. "It burns! But it's cold!"

"It's ginger beer," said Mia.

Rosetta drained her cup and smacked her lips. "Have you got a little something to go with it? A poppy-seed thimblecake,

perhaps? With a dollop of fresh cream
and a sprinkle of pollen?"

Mia studied the cupboard. "We have
cakes," she suggested.

As she handed a piece to Rosetta,
the doorbell rang. Mia ran to answer it.
Her best friend, Kate McCrady, was
standing on the doorstep. Mia had
called Kate and Lainey for help.
She remembered what her mother had
said about not having her friends over.
But this was an emergency.

"You said to come over. Then you said not to come over. Then you said, 'Come over – and hurry!' Make up your mind, Mia!" Kate joked.

Mia didn't feel like laughing. She led Kate into the kitchen. Rosetta was still sitting on the counter, making her way through the cake.

"What are you doing here?" Kate cried when she saw Rosetta. "Aren't we going to Never Land today?"

"Well, that's the thing…." Mia started to explain how Rosetta had ended up on the mainland. But right away Kate interrupted.

"Wait a minute. You mean, you went to Never Land *without* me?" Kate looked both annoyed and envious.

"Don't be mad, Kate," Mia pleaded. "I've got a big problem. Gabby is stuck in Never Land!"

"She went, too? So much for sticking with your friends," Kate grumbled.

To Mia's relief, the doorbell rang again. This time it was Lainey Winters. Her blonde hair was uncombed and her glasses were slightly crooked on her face. "I came as fast as I could," she said breathlessly.

The girls listened as Mia explained how Gabby had come to be trapped in Never Land and Rosetta stuck in their world.

"Can't you do anything?" Lainey asked Rosetta. "I mean, with fairy magic?"

"No, I already asked," Mia told her.

Rosetta lifted her chin. "I'm a garden fairy," she said proudly. "Holes aren't one of my talents. Our magic is different. I can make any flower bloom. I can hear the secrets inside a seed."

Kate rolled her eyes. "A lot of good that will do us."

"You said your dad nailed the board shut," Lainey said, thinking. "So really all we need to do is loosen it again."

"It's nailed down tight," Mia said, "but we can try."

The group hurried outside to study the fence. "Which board was it?" Rosetta asked.

"It was somewhere in the middle," said Mia.

"I thought it was more towards the right," said Kate.

"How can you tell?" asked Lainey. "They all look the same!"

Kate folded her arms across her chest. "Mia should know. *She* was the last one through it," she said, giving Mia a meaningful look.

"Kate, I said I was sorry!" Mia wailed.

"Actually, you didn't," Kate replied.

Mia sighed. "I'm sorry I went to Never Land without you. Will you please stop being mad now?"

"Maybe," Kate said with a smile. She kicked at a few fence boards. "Well, since we can't remember which board it is, I guess we're just going to have to try them all."

"You mean, loosen every board?" Mia was horrified. "What are my parents going to think?"

"What are they going to think when you tell them Gabby sneaked off to the magical island of Never Land while you were supposed to be watching her?" Kate asked pointedly. "Mia, it's the only way."

"Fine." Mia scowled. "I can't wait to get Gabby back ... so I can yell at her."

Kate knelt down and began to wiggle a board. "It's nailed really tight. Ow!" She jerked back her hand. "I got a splinter."

Rosetta fluttered over to her. "Let me see it."

"Do you have healing magic?" Kate asked, holding out her thumb.

"No, but I have tiny hands." Rosetta landed on Kate's palm and began to gently work out the splinter.

That gave Mia an idea. "I know! We need something to pull the nails out." She ran into the house and returned a few moments later with a hammer.

Using the claw end of the hammer, Mia began to wiggle the nail from the wood. "A little more … there!" Mia pulled out the nail, then pushed the board to one side, just enough so she could peek through. "I see flowers. And I can hear water running."

"That must be Havendish Stream!" Rosetta cried joyously. "Oh, I'll be back in time for tea!" She zipped right past Mia and through the gap in the fence.

At that moment, a large shape crossed in front of the gap, blocking Mia's view. She heard someone grumbling. But it didn't sound like a fairy's voice. It sounded like a grown-up.

*That's not Pixie Hollow!* Mia realized with a gasp. It was her neighbour Mrs Peavy's garden – and that large shape blocking her view was Mrs Peavy herself. Rosetta had flown right into the old woman's garden!

"What's wrong, Mia?" Kate asked behind her.

"We got the wrong board." Mia put her eye back to the crack, but she couldn't see the fairy. "Rosetta, come back!" she whispered.

There was no reply.

Mia watched through the crack. She could see Mrs Peavy's feet. The old woman stood still for a long time. She seemed to be looking at something.

Mia's heart beat faster. Had Mrs Peavy found Rosetta?

The old woman turned and walked back towards her house.

As soon as Mrs Peavy was gone, Mia whispered louder, "Rosetta, are you okay?"

Silence.

Mia felt panic rising in her chest. "We have to go in there!" she cried. "Something's happened to Rosetta!"

# Chapter 5

"What do you know about spotting fireflies?" Iridessa asked Gabby.

The two were making their way through the forest just outside Pixie Hollow. Iridessa flew in front of Gabby, leading the way through the moss-covered trees.

"They have lights in their bottoms," Gabby replied.

"That's right," said Iridessa. "But they can be hard to see in the daytime. That's why we need a plan. We should start by looking for puddles. Then we move on to shady thickets. Then we'll go … are you listening, Gabby? Gabby?"

Iridessa turned to look at Gabby, but the little girl had vanished.

Iridessa hovered, looking around. *She's ten times the size of a fairy,* she thought. *How is it possible that I've lost her already?*

"BOO!" Gabby yelled, springing up from behind a bush. Iridessa was so startled that she fell from the air. She landed in a giant fern.

Gabby giggled. "I scared you!"

Iridessa could barely conceal her annoyance. "Gabby, we don't have time for games. Just stay close, okay?"

This time Iridessa flew behind so she could keep an eye on Gabby. But it wasn't easy. The little girl was all over the place! She'd stop to admire a fuzzy caterpillar. Then suddenly she'd dash off to examine a mushroom or peek into a hollow log.

"It's harder than herding a butterfly!" Iridessa groaned.

Before she could stop her, Gabby darted away again. In an instant, she had vanished among the trees.

At last, Iridessa spotted the tips of Gabby's wings poking out from behind a mossy oak. "What are you up to now?" she asked, flying over.

Gabby was holding a silver dandelion. Iridessa watched as she closed her eyes and blew away all the seeds with a single breath. Ever since they'd entered the forest, Gabby had stopped to pick every

dandelion she'd seen. It was starting to drive Iridessa crazy.

"Why do you do that?" she asked.

"For a wish," Gabby said.

"On a dandelion?" Iridessa had never heard of such a thing.

"When you wish on a dandelion, a fairy hears your wish and makes it come true," Gabby replied. "That's what Mia says."

Iridessa frowned. Never fairies didn't grant wishes. In Iridessa's opinion, planning was how you went about making sure things turned out as you wanted. *What a lot of silly ideas Clumsies have,* she thought.

Suddenly, Gabby's eyes lit up. "Ooh, look! A firefly!" She pointed at a glimmer of light ahead in the trees.

A single firefly wasn't worth the trouble of chasing, Iridessa thought. But Gabby was already darting after it. "It's not – wait! Come back!" Iridessa cried.

Gabby scrambled over rocks and under branches, grabbing for the firefly that was always just out of reach. Iridessa was surprised at how fast the girl could run. She could barely keep up.

In moments, they were deep in the woods. The trees grew closer together.

But it wasn't just the trees blocking out the light – the whole forest seemed to be growing darker, almost as if night was drawing in.

*That can't be right,* Iridessa thought. *Sunset is hours away.*

She glanced up at the sky. Between the towering trees, she could see thunderclouds gathering. Storms were rare in Never Land, but they did happen.

Suddenly, Iridessa felt worried. She put on a burst of speed to catch up with Gabby. "Don't go so far. We need to...."

Iridessa trailed off, forgetting the rest of her thought. Gabby was standing in the centre of a clearing, surrounded by thousands of fireflies. They weaved patterns in the air around her. The little girl danced with joy.

Iridessa lived in an enchanted world, but even to her, the scene was like magic. She'd never seen so many fireflies glowing so brightly. For just one moment, Iridessa forgot about her plan and her schedule. She didn't even think of trying to herd all the fireflies. Instead, she flew up next to Gabby. Together, they laughed and danced as the fireflies swirled around them.

Then, all at once, the lights winked out.

"What happened?" Gabby asked.

"Something scared them," Iridessa replied, looking around.

*CRACK!* There came a clap of thunder so loud Iridessa felt it in her bones. The sky opened up and rain poured down. It came down so hard and fast that it washed Iridessa right out of the air.

The fairy landed hard on the muddy ground. She tried to stand and run for shelter. But before she could, a stream of water picked her up and swept her away.

Iridessa bounced over the ground, carried by the water. She grabbed at roots and blades of grass, trying to hold on. But the water tore her away. It swept up everything in its path. Leaves and sticks slammed against her. The forest spun above her. She was going to drown!

Suddenly, a hand grabbed her and lifted her into the air. Iridessa found herself looking into a pair of wide brown eyes.

"Gabby!" Iridessa was so relieved she could have cried.

"Are you okay?" the girl asked.

Iridessa nodded. She was muddy and bruised. Her wings were too wet to fly. But she wasn't badly hurt.

Cradling Iridessa in her hands, Gabby ducked under a giant fern. They waited out the storm. It didn't last long. Almost as quickly as it had come, the rain stopped.

Iridessa fanned her wet wings, trying to dry them. "We'd better go back to Pixie Hollow before we get caught in another storm," she told Gabby. "You'll have to carry me for now. I can't fly with wet wings."

"Okay," said Gabby. "Which way do we go?"

"This way." Iridessa pointed into the trees. "No … that doesn't look right. Is it this way?" She spun in a circle. But each way she turned, the trees looked the same.

With a sinking feeling, Iridessa realized they were lost.

# chapter 6

"Are you sure about this, Kate?" Lainey asked, warily.

Kate was using the hammer to work another nail loose from the fence board. "How else are we going to get into the garden to find Rosetta?" she asked.

"We could ring Mrs Peavy's doorbell," Lainey suggested. "We could say we lost a ball in her garden."

"She'll never let us in," Mia said. "She doesn't even answer the door for Halloween trick-or-treaters. She turns off all the lights and closes her curtains."

"I heard she's a witch," Lainey whispered to her friends.

"I heard that, too," said Mia.

Kate frowned. "I thought witches were supposed to love Halloween." She pulled the nail out. Pushing the board sideways made a gap just big enough to squeeze through.

The girls all looked at each other. "Who's going?" asked Kate. For the first time in her life, she didn't look eager to have an adventure.

"Let's do rock-paper-scissors," Mia suggested. "On the count of three. One … two … three!"

Mia scissored her fingers. Kate and Lainey both curled their fists into rocks.

Mia swallowed hard. "Okay," she said. "Wish me luck."

"Good luck," said Lainey.

"Don't get turned into a frog," said Kate.

Mia scowled at her, then crawled through the fence.

She found herself in an overgrown garden. The grass grew a metre high and the flower beds were choked with weeds. The few flowers that remained were wilted, and the herbs had all gone to seed. The sole tree in the garden was so strangled by ivy that Mia couldn't see any of its bark.

*It sure looks like a witch's garden,* Mia thought. She glanced up at the house, but the curtains were drawn. Was it possible that Rosetta was trapped inside?

Mia tiptoed further into the garden.

Just then, she spotted her friend. The fairy was crouched beside a

bedraggled rosebush. It looked as if she was talking to it.

Mia hurried over. "There you are! We thought something had happened to you. We were so worried!"

Rosetta looked up at her with tears in her eyes. "Mia, look at this  place. Who would do this to a garden? Flowers need love and care. You can't just *ignore* them."

Mia was getting anxious. Mrs Peavy could come back any minute. "We should go now," she whispered.

"But, Mia," Rosetta said, widening her eyes, "I can't *leave* them like this!"

"You there!" a gravelly voice rang out, making Mia's blood run cold. "What are you doing in my garden?"

Mia turned and saw Mrs Peavy standing a few metres away. The woman was wearing a wide-brimmed hat that cast a shadow over the top half of her face, so Mia couldn't see her eyes. But her mouth was turned down in a deep frown. She gripped a gardening trowel in her fist as if it were a weapon.

Mia's lips moved, but no words came out. They seemed to be stuck in her throat.

"Speak up!" Mrs Peavy came closer. Now Mia could see her eyes. They were a startling shade of blue.

"Who were you talking to?" the woman snapped. "And don't lie to me. I can smell a lie a mile away."

*Is that why her nose is so long?* Mia wondered. *For smelling lies?* It seemed like something a witch might be able to do. Mia decided not to take any chances.

"I was talking to a fairy," she answered.

"A fairy?" Mrs Peavy made a sour face. "What nonsense!"

"But it's true!" Mia said. "She's right here!"

"What nonsense!" the woman repeated. "You must be a very silly girl."

"It's no use talking to her," Rosetta said, flying up next to Mia. "Most grown-ups can't see me. You can't see fairies if you don't believe in them."

*How sad,* Mia thought, *not to be able to see magic even when it's right in front of your eyes.* Suddenly, Mrs Peavy didn't seem like a witch. She just seemed like a lonely old woman. A very *grouchy* lonely old woman.

"Now," Mrs Peavy was saying, "what are you going to do about my hollyhocks?"

She pointed at the fence, where a row of unkempt hollyhocks grew. Mia saw that where she'd come through, she'd knocked over a few of the tall flowers. "You'll have to pay for them," her neighbour said.

"But I don't have any money!" Mia exclaimed.

"Then you'll have to work it off," said Mrs Peavy, folding her arms.

Moments later, Mia found herself kneeling on the ground, pulling up weeds in Mrs Peavy's garden. "This is terrible!" Mia whispered to Rosetta. "It will take a hundred years to weed this garden. We're never going to find Gabby. Or get you home again."

"This is my fault," said Rosetta. "If only she would go away!" She frowned at Mrs Peavy, who was sitting on the patio, watching Mia like a hawk.

"You missed a spot!" the old woman called as the phone inside her house started to ring. She got up to answer it.

"It's about time!" Rosetta declared. Without wasting another moment, she began to fly in circles. As she did, the garden started to change.

Weeds shrank. Leaves sprouted. Brown grass turned green again. Wilted flowers straightened and burst into bloom. Round and round Rosetta went, leaving a trail of beauty in her wake. When the entire garden had been transformed, Rosetta flew back to Mia. "There," she said, dusting off her hands. "That's much better."

Just then, Mrs Peavy returned from the house. "I hope you've been pulling up weeds, not ... what on earth?"

She froze at the sight of her beautiful garden and Mia standing in its midst.

"I'm finished, Mrs Peavy," Mia said cheerily. When the woman didn't reply, she added, "I'll just let myself out."

Mia left her neighbour staring in awe, the frown at last wiped off her face.

# chapter 7

When Mia and Rosetta returned to the house, they found Kate and Lainey waiting in the garden. Lainey was biting her nails. Kate was pacing the length of the fence like a tiger in a zoo.

"What took you so long?" Lainey cried when she saw them.

"We thought the witch had got you," Kate added.

"She's not a witch," Mia told them. "She's just a cranky old lady who needed a little bit of magic." She looked at Rosetta, who winked.

"While you were gone, we found something," Lainey reported. She pointed at one of the fence boards. "The nails here are a different colour. They're new!"

"It must be the board your dad fixed," Kate explained. "That means it's the one that leads to Pixie Hollow!"

"Good work, guys," Mia said, picking up the hammer. She felt bad about undoing her father's work. But what choice did she have?

Mia was just working the hammer under the edge of the first nail when the growl of a lawn mower made her jump. She turned to see her father pushing their mower round the side of the house.

Rosetta clapped her hands over her ears. "What is that thing? It's louder than

78

a bullfrog with a bellyache!"

"A lawn mower!" Kate shouted back. "It's for cutting the grass!"

Rosetta made a face. "All that fuss? Over a lawn's haircut?"

"Mia!" her father yelled. He said something else, but the sound of the mower drowned out the rest.

"What?" Mia cried.

Mr Vasquez cut the motor. "I've got to mow the lawn. You girls need to play somewhere else for now." He looked around. "Where's Gabby?"

The girls all spoke at once.

"In the bathroom."

"Hiding."

"Upstairs."

"She's hiding in the bathroom upstairs," Mia said quickly. "We're, er, playing hide-and-seek."

"You'll have to finish your game inside. At least until I'm done out here." Her father reached down and started the mower again.

The girls trudged inside. They watched from the kitchen window as Mia's father pushed the mower back and forth. "At this rate, we'll never get back to Never Land," Kate complained.

On the windowsill, Rosetta was worried. "Isn't there some way we can stop it?" she asked Mia.

Mia shook her head. "Once he starts mowing the lawn, he always finishes. Except...."

"Except what?" asked Lainey.

"Well, I was just thinking of one time when I left a skipping rope on the lawn," Mia explained. "Papi didn't see it and mowed right over it.

The mower jammed. He had to spend the rest of the day fixing it."

"That's what we can do!" Kate said. "We'll jam the mower!"

"No," Mia said firmly. "That's too dangerous. Papi said so. He was really mad last time. But maybe there's another way we can stop it."

Lainey was leaning out of the window and studying the mower. "What's that bag on the back for?" she asked.

"It catches all the grass clippings," Mia said.

"That's what I thought," Lainey said. "Well, what if there was a little hole in the bag. He'd have to stop and fix that, right?"

"So you're saying *we* should put a hole in the bag?" Mia thought about it. "It's not a bad idea."

"Don't you think he'd see us doing something like that?" Kate asked.

"He'd see us," Mia said. "But he wouldn't see Rosetta." The girls all turned to the fairy.

Rosetta's eyes widened. "Oh no, not me! I'm a garden fairy. Holes aren't one of my talents, remember?"

"Please, Rosetta!" Mia said. "We have to get Gabby back. Otherwise, who knows what will happen – the passage to Never Land might stay closed forever! You might never get home."

Rosetta looked from Mia to Lainey to Kate. "To think I went through all this trouble for a pretty dress. Okay, I'll do it," she said with a sigh.

The girls decided that Mia should distract her father while Rosetta made the hole. Mia found a pair of nail scissors in a bathroom drawer. They were small enough for the tiny fairy to carry.

"Be careful," Mia said as she held them out to Rosetta.

Rosetta said nothing, but she took the scissors. Clutching them against her chest, she flew out of the kitchen window into the garden.

After Rosetta was in place, Mia went out of the back door.

"Papi!" Mia shouted.

When her father turned to her, she held up a glass of lemonade. "I thought you might need something to drink."

Her father cut the motor. "Well, that's very nice of you, Mia," he said, taking the glass. Over his shoulder, Mia could see Kate and Lainey watching. But where was Rosetta?

Then Mia spotted her. The fairy was perched on a tulip at the edge of the flower bed.

*Why doesn't she go?* Mia wondered. Then she noticed the flower was trembling. She realized Rosetta was scared!

*Go, Rosetta, go!* Mia silently urged.

After what seemed like an eternity, Rosetta lifted off the flower. She began to fly slowly towards Mia and her dad.

Mr Vasquez finished the lemonade in two big gulps. He handed the glass back to Mia.

"Wait!" Mia cried, stalling for time. "Um ... don't you want some more?"

"Not right now, thanks," her father said. "Maybe when I'm done." He reached down to start the mower.

With a jerk of the cord, the motor roared to life. Her father grabbed the handle of the mower and began to push.

Where was Rosetta? Mia couldn't see her. Had she made the hole? She glanced at the kitchen window. Kate's mouth was a round 'O'. Lainey had her hands over her eyes.

Just then, Mia saw Rosetta. She was clinging to the mower bag as if for dear life. Then Mia's father turned the mower, and Rosetta disappeared from view.

Mia gasped.

Suddenly, a plume of grass clippings shot from the bag like a stream of smoke. Rosetta flew round the side of the mower. She smiled and waved at Mia.

Mia's heart gave a leap. Rosetta had done it!

"What the –" Mia's father stopped the mower. He bent down to examine the bag. Then, grumbling and shaking his head, he rolled the lawn mower back towards the garage.

Now was their chance! Rosetta flew over to Mia as Kate and Lainey hurried outside. The girls met by the fence board.

"Way to go, Rosetta!" Mia said.

"That was cool," Kate agreed. She picked up the hammer, knelt down and began to prise the nail away.

"Hurry, Kate!" Mia crossed her fingers. "If we get Gabby back before Mami comes home, I swear I'll never fight with her again."

"I've ... almost ... got it!" Kate pulled the nail free and the board swung sideways.

"Gabby!" Mia cried, leaning through the fence. "Gabby, we're here –"

Mia broke off. Pixie Hollow wasn't there. Once again, Mia found herself staring at Mrs Peavy's garden.

She knew they'd found the right board this time. But the way back to Never Land was gone!

# Chapter 8

Iridessa scanned the trees, searching for a landmark – a twisted branch, an oddly shaped leaf, *anything* familiar. But in the growing gloom, one tree looked the same as the next.

Iridessa was furious with herself. How could she have got lost? And how could she have come into the forest so unprepared – without food or her basket of sunbeams or even a daisy umbrella to stay dry? It was unlike her to do anything without a plan.

*It's because of Gabby,* Iridessa thought. *I let myself get distracted.* Oh, if only she hadn't agreed to look after her!

But there was nothing she could do about it now. She had to get them both out of the forest.

She fanned her wings and was relieved to discover that they had dried. She fluttered off Gabby's shoulder, where she'd been riding. "Let's hurry," Iridessa urged. "The way back must be somewhere around here."

Gabby didn't seem to hear her. She had stopped to pick another dandelion.

"Come along now, Gabby," Iridessa tried again. "We haven't got time to waste. It will be getting dark soon."

Despite the thick clouds, Iridessa could tell that the sun was lower in the sky. The day was passing quickly and she did not want to spend the night in the forest.

Gabby blew all the seeds off the dandelion, then threw the stem away. "I'm hungry," she said.

"We'll get something good to eat just as soon as we get back to Pixie Hollow," Iridessa promised. "Acorn soup or butter cookies – anything you want!"

"I want something now." A whine crept into Gabby's voice. To Iridessa's dismay, Gabby suddenly sat down.

"We can't stop!" Iridessa wailed. But the girl refused to budge.

Desperately, Iridessa looked around. She spotted a bush a short distance away. It was dotted with tiny fruit. *Blueberries!*

Relieved, Iridessa flew over and plucked two berries from the bush.

She handed one to Gabby. Then she settled on to a tuffet of moss to eat the other one.

As Iridessa bit into the berry, sweet juice filled her mouth. She closed her eyes. *Mmm, that's good!* She hadn't realized how hungry she was. Quickly, she gobbled up the rest.

Iridessa patted her full stomach. Then she caught Gabby's eye. The girl was watching her longingly. It would take more than a single blueberry to fill up a hungry Clumsy, Iridessa realized.

She led Gabby to the berry bush and hovered anxiously as Gabby ate her fill. Just as Gabby finished, there was another clap of thunder. The rain began to fall again.

This time they found shelter in a mossy hollow log. As they huddled together, Iridessa stared out at the rain.

She was tired, cold, dirty and damp. She didn't know what to do. The other fairies were all so busy, Iridessa knew it would be at least another day before anyone thought to look for them.

"Tell me a story, Iridessa," Gabby said, looking out at the rain.

"We haven't got time for –" Iridessa broke off. Right now, time was all they had. They couldn't go anywhere until the rain stopped. She searched her brain for a story but found only worries. "I can't think of one. Why don't you tell me a story instead?"

"All right." Gabby thought for a moment. "Once upon a time, there was a fairy who lived in a place called Pixie Hollow."

"What was the fairy's name?" asked Iridessa.

"Iridessa," Gabby said without a moment's hesitation.

Iridessa smiled. "That's a good name."

"Iridessa was friends with a girl," Gabby went on. "They were very best friends. They did all sorts of stuff together."

"What kind of stuff?" Iridessa asked.

"Like once when they went into the woods. At first the girl was a little bit scared because it was dark, but then Iridessa showed her firefly magic. And when they got hungry, Iridessa made a blueberry bush grow."

"I didn't –" Iridessa stopped. It was just a story, after all. "Then what happened?"

Gabby yawned. "Um … then they went home and had hot chocolate," she murmured. Her eyelids were growing heavy. "The end."

The rain drummed on the hollow log. Iridessa felt herself getting sleepy, too. She brightened her glow to try to stay awake. "Everything will be okay, Gabby," she said. "We'll get home soon."

"I know," Gabby said as her eyes closed. "Because you have fairy magic." A moment later, she was asleep.

Iridessa sat watching her. She had never known anyone, fairy or Clumsy, who had so much faith in fairy magic. Gabby thought Iridessa could do anything.

*If only it were true,* Iridessa thought. *If only I had the right magic to help us now.*

# chapter 9

Warm sunlight touched Iridessa's face. She opened her eyes. She was lying at the entrance to the hollow log. Outside, the rain had stopped. Rays of morning sunlight shone down through the trees, making the wet forest sparkle.

Iridessa sat up quickly as she remembered that they were lost. *How could I have fallen asleep?* She turned to wake Gabby. But the log was empty.

Iridessa flew outside. She spotted the little girl a short distance away.

Gabby was staring at something in the trees.

She smiled as Iridessa flew up to her. "Look," she said, pointing.

A trail of dandelions led through the forest. All Gabby's wishes hadn't been for nothing after all, Iridessa realized. They had left a path of seeds behind them – and after the rain, the flowers had sprouted. Their yellow dandelion heads pointed the way home. *There must have been some magic in those wishes for the flowers to sprout so quickly*, Iridessa thought.

"Oh, you clever girl!" Iridessa cried. *All this time I thought I was taking care of Gabby*, she mused. *But really, she's been taking care of me.*

"If we hurry, we'll be back in time for breakfast," Iridessa said. "Come on, Gabby. I'll race you!"

Iridessa and Gabby arrived back in Pixie Hollow to find everything ready for a party. Colourful paper lanterns hung from the branches of the Home Tree. Walnuts roasted on spits over tiny fires, and barrels of honeysuckle punch stood around the courtyard. The sound of musicians tuning their finger harps drifted through the air.

Iridessa's first thought was that Pixie Hollow was holding a party to welcome them home. Then she realized the fairies must have finished fixing the bridge during the night. The party was to celebrate the bridge's reopening.

"Ah, home!" Iridessa exclaimed. The smell of the walnuts made her mouth water. "Come on. Let's get something to eat."

Gabby didn't reply. She looked around with a forlorn expression. Suddenly, a tear rolled down her cheek.

"What's wrong?" Iridessa asked. She didn't understand why Gabby was crying.

"My wish didn't come true," Gabby said, then burst into tears.

Iridessa had been so happy to be back that she'd forgotten about Gabby's problem. Now she remembered how far the girl was from her own home. "Did you wish the hole would be fixed?" she asked gently.

"No." Gabby sniffled. "I wished Mia wouldn't be mad at me any more. I wished she would be right here in Pixie Hollow waiting for me. But she didn't come. She doesn't care about me."

"Oh, Gabby, of course she does," Iridessa said.

Gabby shook her head. "She says I mess everything up."

"You don't mess everything up," Iridessa said. "You're the one who got us back to Pixie Hollow. And you rescued me from the flood. And you're the one who found all the fireflies in the forest. You did everything right. You are sweet and brave and imaginative. I would be glad if you were my sister."

Iridessa realized that it was true. If it weren't for Gabby, she never would have seen the dancing fireflies or the trail of wishes. Those things hadn't been part of her plan, but Iridessa wouldn't have wanted to miss them for the world.

Gabby had her own kind of magic, she thought. And in its way, it was as powerful as any fairy magic.

But Iridessa's words didn't seem to comfort Gabby. The tears continued to trickle down her face.

Nearby, a silver dandelion was growing in the grass. Half-heartedly, Gabby plucked it and blew away its seeds. "I want to go home," she said.

*

On the other side of the fence, Mia clutched her head. "It didn't work!" she cried. "Why didn't it work?"

"Let me try," Kate said. She swung the board shut, then pulled it open again. But all they saw was the neighbour's garden.

"So I can't ever get home again." Rosetta slumped. In the wrinkled doll's dress, she looked like a wilted flower. Mia felt terrible. Just a few hours before, it had seemed like so much fun to have a fairy living in her doll's house. But now that it was about to come true, it felt like a tragedy.

Tears pricked Mia's eyes. "I'm so sorry, Rosetta. It's all my fault. I never should have brought you here. I should have been watching Gabby."

Mia thought of Gabby that morning. How she'd wanted to play a game. *If only I'd played with her!* Mia thought. Now she might never have the chance to play with her sister again.

Mia wasn't worried about getting in trouble with her parents. She wasn't thinking of how she'd tell Gabby off. She just wanted her sister back.

Through the screen of her tears, Mia saw something white drifting through the air. *Snowflakes – in summertime?*

Mia wiped her eyes. But then she saw that they weren't snowflakes after all. They were dandelion seeds.

Lainey and Kate noticed them, too. "Where did those come from?" Kate wondered aloud.

Rosetta caught one of the silky seeds. She pressed it to her ear and her eyes widened. "This seed is from Never Land!"

Mia leaped to her feet. "Are you sure? How do you know?"

Rosetta lifted her chin. "I told you, I can hear the secrets inside a seed. It's what garden fairies do."

More dandelion seeds drifted down through the air. Mia looked up and saw that they were coming from Gabby's open bedroom window.

The girls all looked at each other. "Do you think...?" Kate began.

"That the hole moved?" Lainey nodded. "It's possible."

"Anything is possible in Never Land," Mia agreed.

The girls raced into the house, with Rosetta flying behind. Mia took the stairs two at a time. When she opened the door to Gabby's room, she saw dandelion seeds drifting from beneath the wardrobe door.

Mia held her breath, hardly daring to hope. She put her hand on the doorknob.

When she pulled the door open, she felt a warm breeze against her face. She smelled orange blossoms and sun-warmed moss.

Mia stepped through the door, crying, "Gabby! We're coming!"

# chapter 10

As Mia went through the dark wardrobe, she had a moment of doubt. What if the opening had moved on the Never Land side, too? What if it led to a pirate's ship or a dragon's lair rather than Pixie Hollow?

But a second later, Mia and her friends emerged into sunlight. They were standing on the bank of Havendish Stream. From across the stream, they could hear the lively sound of fairy music.

"I'm home! Oh, it's so good to be back!" Rosetta exclaimed. She did a joyous twirl in the air, then darted away without a backwards glance.

*She didn't even say goodbye,* thought Mia. But she didn't have time to dwell on that because just ahead, standing in the Home Tree courtyard, was her sister.

"Gabby!" Mia splashed through the stream, not caring that her feet got wet. A moment later, she had wrapped her sister in a hug so tight that Gabby was lifted right off the ground.

"You came!" Gabby exclaimed, hugging her sister back.

"Of course I came!" Mia said. "We've been trying to get here all day."

"So you're not mad at me?" Gabby asked as Mia set her down.

"Mad? I'm furious with you!" Mia exclaimed, giving her sister another big hug. This time Kate and Lainey joined in.

"I thought you closed the hole because you were mad at me," Gabby said.

"What? No!" Mia laughed. "We couldn't get here because Papi fixed the fence."

"And when we got the board loose again, the hole was gone!" Lainey explained.

"But you'll never believe where it showed up!" Kate jumped in. "*Your* room, Gabby! You're so lucky. You can go to Never Land any time you want, day or night."

"No she can't!" Mia said quickly. "You're not allowed to go to Never Land without me."

"Or me," said Kate.

"Or me," added Lainey. "But I still don't understand why the hole moved."

Iridessa suddenly spoke up. "Never Land must want you here."

All the girls turned to the fairy, who was hovering next to Gabby. "What do you mean? Never Land is just an island," Kate pointed out. "How can it want something?"

"It's an island with a mind of its own," Iridessa said. "Have you ever heard the expression 'When one knothole closes, another one opens'?"

"It's 'When one *door* closes, another one opens'," Lainey said.

"Door. Knothole." Iridessa shrugged. "Never Land must have opened a path for you to reach it. It's the only explanation I can think of."

Mia noticed how Iridessa hovered near Gabby's shoulder. She didn't seem to want to leave her side. Mia was about to ask what Never Land wanted them for, but at that moment, Rosetta came flying back. Tinker Bell was with her.

"I told Tink all about the grass machine and the hole I put in it," she said. "She thinks she can fix it."

Tinker Bell looked excited. "It sounds like an interesting case."

"It didn't seem right to leave it for your father to fix," Rosetta explained.

"Are you sure it's a good idea to come back with us?" Mia asked. "What if the hole closes again and you get stuck like Rosetta did?"

Tink puffed her chest out bravely. "I've been to the mainland before. I can manage."

"But you must stay for the bridge-opening party!" Rosetta clapped her hands. "A party at last! I wonder what I should wear?" She looked down at the doll's dress, which was looking bedraggled after her adventure on the mainland. "It's a shame about this one, after all that trouble."

"We can't stay for the party. What about your mum?" Lainey reminded Mia.

"Oh! That's right. Mami is coming home any minute. We have to get back right away!" Mia grabbed Gabby's hand.

Gabby dug in her heels. "No, I want to stay."

"Gabby...." Mia warned. And just like that, the two sisters began arguing again.

At last, Mia convinced Gabby to go home, swearing that they would return to Pixie Hollow as soon as they could. They said their goodbyes to Rosetta and Iridessa. Then, with Tink flying alongside them, the girls headed back to the hollow tree.

Before she ducked inside, Mia turned for one last look at Pixie Hollow. She took in the flowers, the music and the beautiful Home Tree, trying to tuck it all away in her memory. Mia was sure that they would be back – almost sure, anyway. But she wanted to remember everything, just in case.

Then Mia turned towards the hole that led back home. As she stepped through, she took Gabby's hand tightly in her own.

Don't miss the next magical
book in the Never Girls series!

Kate McCrady opened one eye, then the other. Early-morning sunlight streamed across her face.

Kate blinked, still half asleep. Was she in her own bedroom? Was she sleeping under the weeping willow tree in Never Land? For a moment, she didn't know. She pushed a tangle of red hair out of the way and saw a large doll's house in the corner.

*Oh, that's right,* Kate thought. She was at her best friend Mia Vasquez's house, sleeping over. Lainey Winters was there, too, bundled in a sleeping bag a few metres away.

Kate tried to send them a silent message: *Wake up! Wake up, so we can go back!*

Only a few days before, Kate, Mia, Lainey and Mia's little sister, Gabby, had found a secret portal to Pixie Hollow, the realm of the fairies on the island of Never Land. Or rather, the portal had found them – even though the path to Never Land wasn't always in the same place, it always seemed to be where the girls could find it.

Kate loved their visits to Never Land. There she had no homework, no chores – nothing to do but explore. Adventure waited round every tree, hill and bend along Havendish Stream. Kate couldn't wait to go back.

But her silent message didn't work. Lainey let out a gentle snore. Mia turned over, burrowing deeper under her covers.

Maybe a nudge would wake them. Kate stretched so her foot grazed the bottom of Lainey's sleeping bag. She scooted closer, then stretched again. This time, she bumped Lainey's leg.

Lainey sat up, blinking sleepily.

"I was just stretching," said Kate, trying to look innocent. "I didn't wake you, did I?"

"No … yes." Lainey fumbled around by her pillow. When she found her glasses, she put them on a little crookedly. "Is Mia awake?"

"I am now!" cried Mia, pulling the pillow over her head. Kate could only see a bit of her long, dark curly hair poking out. "What time is it? It feels too early to be awake."

"It *is* early." Kate jumped up, leaped over Lainey and bounced on Mia's bed. "Early enough to get back to Never Land."

Mia glanced at the clock. It said 6:30. "My parents won't be awake until at least seven."

"Exactly," said Kate. "And that could mean hours and hours in Never Land." The girls had discovered that time worked differently on their trips to Pixie Hollow. Hours could pass there, while at home hardly a minute would go by. "Let's go now!"